TIMOTHY

DUMBO

This high-flying book belongs to:

THE RINGMASTER

MRS. JUMBO

Published by Scholastic Inc.,
90 Old Sherman Turnpike, Danbury, Connecticut 06816.

For information regarding permission, write to:
Disney Licensed Publishing,
114 Fifth Avenue, New York, New York 10011.

0-7172-8701-7

Printed in the U.S.A.
First printing, November 2006

Walt Disney's DUMBO

SCHOLASTIC INC.

New York Toronto London Auckland Sydney
Mexico City New Delhi Hong Kong Buenos Aires

The circus had rested all winter, but now spring had come. The performers were rehearsing their new acts, and everyone was looking forward to touring the country.

But many of the animals had more to look forward to than just performing. They were particularly excited, because they were expecting a delivery from the stork!

It happened in the middle of the night. A flock of storks, each with a little bundle in its beak, caught sight of the circus train below.

From the sky, the storks all dropped the bundles with baby animals inside. The bundles drifted down by parachute.

The bear got two babies, the kangaroo got one baby, the hippopotamus got one, the giraffe got one—and the tiger family got three!

Everyone was happy. Well, almost everyone.

Mrs. Jumbo didn't get a baby, and she was sure that it was her turn.

The next morning, the circus train was ready to leave. Poor Mrs. Jumbo was still looking up in the sky. She thought her stork had forgotten about her.

"All aboard!" called the ringmaster, and the train took off.

On a small cloud, a stork was sitting studying a map, looking for the circus. He had one more baby to deliver. His bundle was so heavy that it almost fell through the cloud!

Suddenly he spotted the circus train. A moment later he landed on top of it.

"Mrs. Jumbo!" he called.

"Yoo-hoo! Over here!" the female elephants shouted. They put their trunks up through a hatch in the roof.

The stork jumped down to the elephants,
and Mrs. Jumbo received her bundle.
    "What's his name?" asked the stork.
    "Jumbo Junior," replied Mrs. Jumbo.

Mrs. Jumbo was so happy. She just couldn't wait to see what was inside the package.

When the bundle was opened, everyone thought the baby was adorable. Then he sneezed . . . and his ears came tumbling down around him.

"Oh! Is it possible?" asked one of the elephants.
"Isn't there some mistake? Just look at those
EARS!" The other elephants laughed.

Mrs. Jumbo stepped in to defend her baby. One of the other elephants was very mean and said that the baby looked so dumb that he should just be called "Dumbo."

Mrs. Jumbo stopped paying attention to what they were saying. There was nothing wrong with her baby! She took her tired little son and rocked him to sleep.

In the middle of the night, the train arrived at its first stop. Even though the rain was pouring down, the strong men and the big elephants began the tough work of getting the tent up.

The next afternoon, the entire
circus paraded through town.
The proud ringmaster rode in
front on a white horse.

At the end of the elephant line was Dumbo,
with a small doll on his back. He was very excited
but unfortunately he slipped on one of his big
ears and fell into a puddle!

Later, a group of boys teased Dumbo and pulled his ears.

Mrs. Jumbo was very angry. She lifted one of the troublemakers up, put him over the rope barrier, and slapped him on his backside with her trunk.

"Hey! Cut that out!" the boy yelled. "Help!"

But Mrs. Jumbo just grew more upset. All the circus people rushed in with ropes to try to stop Mrs. Jumbo.

Soon Mrs. Jumbo was chained to the wall in a train car—all by herself. She felt as if she were in jail. Worst of all, she couldn't see Dumbo.

All the other elephants were sure that Dumbo was to blame. They thought he brought misfortune to the circus. They turned their backs on him.

Dumbo went outside. He was very sad. He felt all alone in the world.

Timothy, a circus mouse, had seen and heard everything.

"Poor little guy," he said. Then he decided to do something about it. He marched right up to the elephants.

"AAAHH!" they screamed when they saw the mouse.

Timothy found Dumbo hiding in a haystack. "Hey, Dumbo! You can come out now," said Timothy. "I'm your friend."

Using a peanut, Timothy tried to tempt Dumbo to come out.

"I think your ears are beautiful," Timothy told him.

As the new friends walked past the
ringmaster's tent, they overheard a conversation.
    "Have I got an idea!" said the ringmaster. "One
elephant climbs on top of another elephant until
finally all seventeen elephants have constructed
an enormous pyramid of pachyderms! And now
comes the climax!"
    But the ringmaster couldn't think of a climax.
He hoped it would come
to him in a dream, so he
went to bed.
    Suddenly, Timothy
had an idea!

When the ringmaster was fast asleep, Timothy sneaked into the tent and crawled up to his bed. Timothy hid underneath the sheet, leaned towards the ringmaster's ear, and whispered: "I am the voice of your inspiration. Now concentrate . . ."

"Now you are getting that climax," Timothy continued. "And who is it? The little elephant with the big ears—Dumbo!"

The ringmaster awoke with a start. "I've got it! I've got it!" he said.

All day long, the elephants practiced.

Finally it was time for the big show. They succeeded in balancing on top of each other.

"Ladies and gentlemen,"
the ringmaster shouted.
"I give you *DUMBO!*"

A drum roll echoed from the
orchestra. Dumbo ran toward
the springboard with a small
flag in his trunk.

But poor Dumbo slipped on his ears
again and slammed into the ball that the
elephants were balancing on.

The pachyderm pyramid collapsed—and so did the circus tent! The audience fled.

Back in the elephants' train car, a female elephant told the others the latest news about Dumbo: "Well, they've gone and made him a clown."

"Oh, the shame of it!" said an elderly female elephant. "Let us take a solemn vow. From now on, he is no longer an elephant." And the bruised and bandaged elephants once again turned their backs on little Dumbo.

Dumbo was indeed a clown. He had to pretend to be a baby, jumping from a burning house. The clowns were pretending to catch him, but he landed in a tub filled with whipped cream.

The clowns and the audience thought it was great fun.

Dumbo didn't think so. He was very unhappy.

Timothy comforted him and helped him wash off the whipped cream. To cheer Dumbo up, Timothy said, "Come on. We're going to see your mother!"

The two friends headed over to the train car, where Mrs. Jumbo was still in chains.

DANGER!

MAD ELEPHANT!

KEEP OUT!

Mrs. Jumbo
recognized her
son's trunk at once,
and Dumbo was
overjoyed. Timothy
looked on proudly.

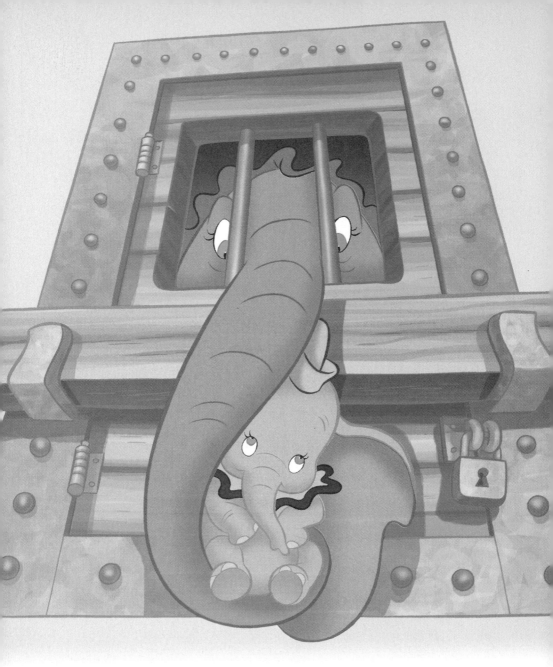

Through the bars, Mrs. Jumbo was able to cuddle
her little son and give him a swing in her trunk.

At the same time, there was a party going on in the clowns' tent. They were so happy with their new firemen's act that they celebrated late into the night.

Meanwhile, after a long day, Dumbo was exhausted. He dreamed that he was flying!

The next morning, Dumbo and Timothy awoke to the noise from some crows above them.

"My, my! I can't believe my eyes!" said one crow.

He was looking at Dumbo and Timothy. They were up in a tree!

"Dumbo," Timothy whispered. "I think we're up in a tree!"

Dumbo's eyes widened. He looked down . . . and lost his balance.

SPLASH! They landed in the middle of a pond. The crows laughed and laughed at the very wet pair.

"I wonder how we got up in that tree, anyway," said Timothy.

"Hey! Maybe you flew up," teased one of the crows.

"That's it!" Timothy exclaimed. "Dumbo, you flew! Your ears! Why, they're perfect wings!"

They went up to a cliff.
The crows suggested using a
"magic" feather to help make
Dumbo think he could fly.

"Let's go, Dumbo!" said Timothy, as Dumbo ran. "Faster, faster!"

Soon he was flying!

"Look! You're flying! You're flying!" cried Timothy. "Wait till we get to the big town!"

For that night's clown act, the burning house was built higher than ever. A drum roll began . . . .

Timothy, who was sitting in Dumbo's hat, whispered, "Dumbo, you're on the threshold of success!"

Dumbo jumped, and the "magic" feather accidentally flew away!

Timothy panicked. "Open up your ears," he told Dumbo. "You can still fly. The feather was just a gag!"

Just before Dumbo hit the ground, he spread his ears, and they sailed through the air.

People shouted in surprise and applauded. They had never seen a flying elephant before! The clowns jumped into the tub as Dumbo passed by.

Now Dumbo was famous! Best of all, the circus workers released Mrs. Jumbo from her chains. She was so proud of her famous son! Now Dumbo had his very own train car, which he shared with his mother . . . and Timothy, of course!

EYE SPY

Look back in the story and try to find these images.